Dear Parents and Educators,

Welcome to Penguin Young Readers! As parents and educators, you know that each child develops at his or her own pace—in terms of speech, critical thinking, and, of course, reading. Penguin Young Readers recognizes this fact. As a result, each Penguin Young Readers book is assigned a traditional easy-to-read level (1–4) as well as a Guided Reading Level (A–P). Both of these systems will help you choose the right book for your child. Please refer to the back of each book for specific leveling information. Penguin Young Readers features esteemed authors and illustrators, stories about favorite characters, fascinating nonfiction, and more!

Farm Days

LEVEL 2

GUIDED READING LEVEL **I**

This book is perfect for a **Progressing Reader** who:
- can figure out unknown words by using picture and context clues;
- can recognize beginning, middle, and ending sounds;
- can make and confirm predictions about what will happen in the text; and
- can distinguish between fiction and nonfiction.

Here are some **activities** you can do during and after reading this book:
- Make Connections: In this story, Chip lives in the city, and he visits his cousins who live on a farm. Life on the farm is very different from Chip's life in the city. Have you ever visited friends or relatives who lived very differently than you? Write a paragraph about your experience and what you learned.
- Research: Chip learns all about what life is like on a farm. Do some of your own research on one aspect of what Chip learned: gardening, mowing hay, or milking cows. What did you learn about farm life?

Remember, sharing the love of reading with a child is the best gift you can give!

—Bonnie Bader, EdM
  Penguin Young Readers program

*Penguin Young Readers are leveled by independent reviewers applying the standards developed by Irene Fountas and Gay Su Pinnell in *Matching Books to Readers: Using Leveled Books in Guided Reading*, Heinemann, 1999.

PENGUIN YOUNG READERS
Published by the Penguin Group
Penguin Group (USA) LLC, 375 Hudson Street, New York, New York 10014, USA

USA | Canada | UK | Ireland | Australia | New Zealand | India | South Africa | China

penguin.com
A Penguin Random House Company

Library of Congress Cataloging-in-Publication Data is available.

ISBN 978-0-448-48230-9 (pbk)   10 9 8 7 6 5 4 3 2 1
ISBN 978-0-8037-3936-9 (hc)   10 9 8 7 6 5 4 3 2 1

PENGUIN YOUNG READERS

LEVEL
PROGRESSING
READER
2

Farm Days

by William Wegman

Penguin Young Readers
An Imprint of Penguin Group (USA) LLC

City boy Chip was going to visit

his country cousins,

Batty and Crooky.

They said they were going

to meet him at the train.

But they were not there.

His cousins must be busy

at the farm.

So Chip decided to walk.

Which way was the farm?

This way?

No.

Maybe it was that way.

Chip was not sure.

But then Chip

saw a cow.

He must be close.

Chip saw a farmer sitting

in a barn window.

"I'm looking for

Batty and Crooky," Chip said.

"Is this their farm?"

It was!

Chip was in the right place.

"Your cousins are out

in the big field,"

the farmer said.

"They are planting a garden.

Hop on!

Let's go see them."

Chip found his cousins,

Batty and Crooky.

"Hi, Chip," said Batty.

"Hi, Chip," said Crooky.

They were very happy to see Chip.

They were sorry they hadn't come

to the station.

They had to work in the garden.

"There is a lot to do on the farm,"

said Crooky.

"We need your help," said Batty.

Chip got the wheelbarrow
and shovel.

They went to the garden.

In one row,

they planted broccoli.

In another row,

they planted radishes.

In another row,

they planted squash.

Crooky said to plant tomatoes
to the left.

He said to plant onions in the back.

Or maybe it was
the other way around.

Crooky couldn't remember.

Chip dug the garden.

He pulled out all the heavy rocks.

He set up a fence.

Batty and Crooky

planted the seeds.

"Make sure you give your garden

plenty of water," the farmer said.

The farmer showed them

his garden.

They saw giant carrots.

And jumbo squash.

How did the farmer

grow healthy vegetables?

"You have to know the four *W*s," the farmer said.

"Water,

 weed,

and wait."

"That's only three," said Chip.

"Whatever," said the farmer.

"Oh," said Chip.

"Water, weed, wait, and whatever."

Chip wanted to pull weeds.

But there was no time for that.

A cow mooed.

"Would you like to milk a cow,

Chip?" the farmer asked.

"I like milk," said Chip.

But Chip did not milk the cow.

Instead, the farmer gave them

some milk to drink.

Then it was time for lunch.

After lunch, the farmer

took them to the big field.

"Chip can mow the hay,"

the farmer said.

Batty and Crooky showed Chip

how to mow.

"You just push," said Batty.

"And keep pushing," said Crooky.

Chip pushed and pushed.

Batty and Crooky went

to the pond.

They checked on the ducks.

They checked on the fish.

Chip continued to mow and mow
and mow, mow, mow, mow, mow.

Later, the farmer heard a

strange sound.

"What is that noise?"

the farmer asked.

"Is it bumblebees?"

No, it was Chip!

He had fallen asleep

in a soft pile of hay.

"Wake up!" the farmer said.

"There is no time for naps.

There is still work to do."

The farmer gave Chip a hat

to put on his head.

Chip had a new job.

"I don't see any crows," Chip said.

"He is doing a good job,"
said Batty.

"Chip looks really scary," said Crooky.

Chip was very tired.

Farming was hard work!

It was time for him to go home.

Batty and Crooky and the farmer

were sad to see Chip leave.

Chip waved good-bye

and told them all thank you.

He had learned a lot

about farming.

"Come back soon," said Batty

and Crooky.

After he got home,

Chip sent a letter

to his cousins

and the farmer.

"Thank you for letting me

visit you on your farm," he wrote.

"I have a new job.

I am a drummer.

Please visit me in the city."

Chip added, "How's the garden?

Don't forget to water,

or whatever!"